PETE
SAMPRAS

*(Photo on
front cover.)*

**Sampras
returns a ball
in the 1993
French Open.**

*(Photo on
previous pages.)*

**Sampras
defeats David
Wheaton in
the Lipton
Championships.**

Photography supplied by Wide World Photos Inc.

Library of Congress Catalog-in-Publication Data
Rambeck, Richard.
Pete Sampras / Richard Rambeck
p. cm.
Summary: Follows the career of the professional tennis player
who had won three Wimbledon championships by the
age of twenty-four.
ISBN 1-56766-262-5 (Lib. Bdg.)

1. Sampras, Pete — Juvenile literature.
2. Tennis players — United States — Biography — Juvenile
lierature. [1. Sampras. Pete. 2. Tennis players.]
I. Title
GV994.S16R68   1997   95-42610
796.342'092 — dc20   CIP
[B]   AC

PETE
SAMPRAS

BY RICHARD RAMBECK

Sampras backhands a return in the 1994 U.S. Open.

Back and forth went the tennis ball. Over the net and back. On and on. Andre Agassi would hit a great shot, and Pete Sampras would run the ball down and return it to Agassi's side of the net. It was the longest point of the match—and one of the greatest points in tennis history. Agassi hit his eleventh and final shot of the rally. Then Sampras made his eleventh and final return of the point. It was a brilliant backhand shot across the court, and Agassi couldn't return it.

The point was finally over, and so was the first set of the 1995 U.S. Open men's singles championship match. Sampras's backhand return had won him the first set. "That's the best point I've ever been a part of," said Sampras, who took the first set six games to four. He wound up winning the match three sets to one, and beating Agassi, who was the world's No. 1 ranked player. For Sampras, who was ranked second, it was his third U.S. Open singles title. He had also won in 1990 and 1993.

Even though Sampras captured the 1995 U.S. Open, Agassi kept his No. 1 ranking. That didn't matter to Sampras. "I don't think people are going to remember who was ranked No. 1 in 1995," he said. "I think they're going to remember who won the major tournaments"—and

President George Bush teams up with Pete Sampras.

Pete Sampras warms up for his second round match in the 1994 French Open.

that was Sampras. In 1995, he not only won the U.S. Open, he also took the All-England singles title at Wimbledon. The Wimbledon win was his third in a row. He is the only U.S. male player to have done that.

"Wimbledon is my favorite," Sampras said after winning the 1995 tournament. "I'd say for 90 percent of us, that's the one tournament we want to win." Sampras beat German star Boris Becker in the final, winning three out of four sets. Becker just couldn't handle Sampras's powerful serve, which flies across the net at speeds up to 129 miles per hour. "You just hope for rain," Becker said of the best way to deal with those serves.

Boris Becker knows something about winning Wimbledon. He took the singles title himself in 1985, 1986, and 1989. He lost in the finals in 1990, 1991, and to Sampras in 1995. "It used to be mine," Becker said of the Wimbledon tournament. "Now it's his." When the match ended, a happy Sampras ripped off his shirt and threw it into the crowd. "It's history, baby," Sampras said of his third straight Wimbledon title.

During the two-week Wimbledon tournament, Sampras did little except eat, sleep, and play tennis. He left his hotel room only to practice and play matches, or to grab a sandwich. He want-

Sampras wins his first Wimbledon Championship, in 1993.

JERABEK SCHOOL
10050 Avenida Magnifica
San Diego, CA 92131
578-5330

ed to remain focused on his goal of winning the championship. But once he had the title, Sampras was ready to enjoy his victory. "There is no better feeling than waking up after winning one of these—if I ever get to sleep," he joked.

Pete Sampras celebrated his 24th birthday a couple of weeks before the 1995 U.S. Open. Even at that young age, he had already become one of the most successful U.S. men's tennis players of all time. He had won seven major tournament titles: three Wimbledons, three U.S. Opens, and the 1994 Australian Open. Sampras had already claimed more U.S.

Open titles than had his idol, Australian star Rod Laver, a great player in the 1960s.

Sampras grew up wanting to be the best player in the world. When he was only seven years old, he dreamed he was No. 1. Sixteen years later, he was! When Sampras was 19, he won the U.S. Open for the first time, beating fellow American Andre Agassi in the finals. The experts said Sampras was headed for great things. He was, but not right away. A year and a half later, in December 1991, Sampras was struggling with his game.

Sampras hadn't won a major tournament since the 1990 U.S. Open. He decided he needed some help. He asked

Tom Gullikson, a former top U.S. singles player, to be his new coach. Gullikson, however, was already busy coaching other players. Plus, he was captain of the U.S. Davis Cup team. Gullikson had an idea, though. "Listen," he said to Sampras, "I know a guy who looks just like me. He talks maybe a little more, but he thinks exactly like me."

Tom Gullikson's "guy" was his twin brother, Tim. With Tim Gullikson's help, Sampras went from being the sixth-ranked player in the world to No. 1. In January 1995, during the Australian Open, Gullikson began to feel very dizzy. He was rushed to the hospital, where he stayed for several days before going back to the United States. Sampras was by his side almost constantly for four days. During his third-round match against Jim Courier, Sampras started to cry. He was thinking of his coach.

Sampras defeats Kevin Ollyet.

He thought I was going to die," said Gullikson, who was suffering from a brain tumor. Despite his tears, Sampras fought through them to beat Courier. He reached the finals, where he lost to Agassi. After he won Wimbledon in 1995, Sampras called it an emotional victory "because of the way the year has gone."

Sampras makes a return to Roger Smith.

After winning the U.S. Open, Sampras looked into a television camera and said, "That's for you, Timmy."

At his home near Chicago, Gullikson watched proudly as his pupil won another major title. The victory didn't make Sampras the top-ranked player in the world—Agassi was still No. 1. But Pete Sampras did prove that he was the best at winning the big tournament. "Every time you hold that trophy up, it's a great feeling," said the three-time U.S. Open and Wimbledon champion. "Let's hope it happens again." There's no doubt that it will.

F